Balboa Press books may be ordered through booksellers or by contacting:

Balboa Press
A Division of Hay House
1663 Liberty Drive
Bloomington, IN 47403
www.balboapress.com
1 (877) 407-4847

Because of the dynamic nature of the Internet, any web addresses or links contained in this book may have changed since publication and may no longer be valid. The views expressed in this work are solely those of the author and do not necessarily reflect the views of the publisher, and the publisher hereby disclaims any responsibility for them.

Any people depicted in stock imagery provided by Thinkstock are models, and such images are being used for illustrative purposes only.
Certain stock imagery © Thinkstock.

ISBN: 978-1-5043-4688-7 (sc)
ISBN: 978-1-5043-4689-4 (e)

Library of Congress Control Number: 2015920816

Print information available on the last page.

Balboa Press rev. date: 01/04/2016

BALBOA.
PRESS
A DIVISION OF HAY HOUSE

Gregory Gregory

Hates His Food

Written and Illustrated by

Muffy Kashkin Grollier

Gregory,
Gregory
hates
his food.

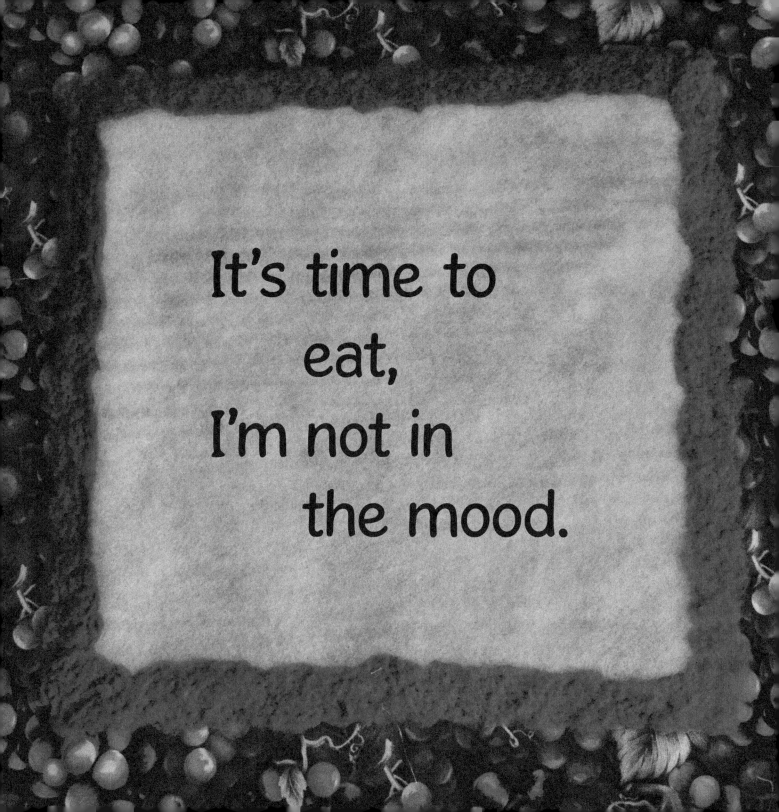

It's time to
eat,
I'm not in
the mood.

He hates fish
He hates meat.
"Don't want
spinach,
I won't eat!"

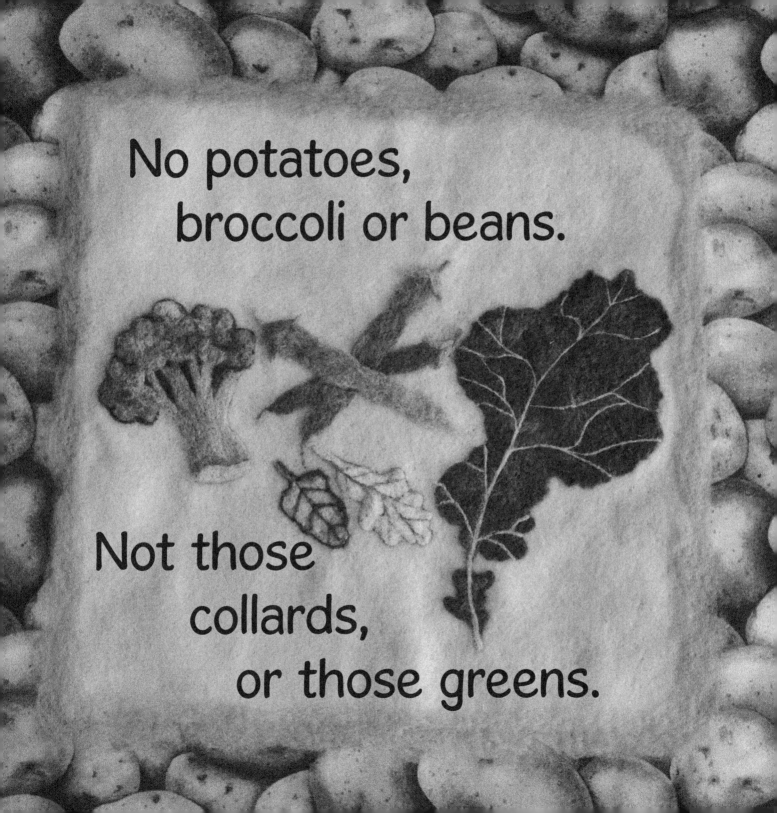

No potatoes,
   broccoli or beans.

Not those
   collards,
      or those greens.

He hates turnips,
carrots and peas.

Won't eat
cucumber,

Not that beet.

No more food,
I won't eat.

Then one day
His new teeth
grew.
He could bite,
He could
chew!

He eats breakfast,
dinner and lunch.

Eats his carrots
by the bunch.

He eats fruit,
vegetables too.

Eats his meat,
since his new teeth
grew

Mom is happy
Gregory eats,

Meals and snacks,
And special treats

Strong young bones, healthy weight.

Because
Gregory,
Gregory
Cleans
his
plate.